Miss Cornett's Courtship

by

Cate Neilson

Miss Cornett's Courtship (c) Catelyn Neilson Cover and Text Design (c) Catelyn Neilson

ISBN: 978-0-359-44020-7

Library of Congress Catalog Card Number: 97-97200

504 1/4 Vine St.

Paris, KY 40361

Dedication

For my Mother, Sylvia...

thank you for the legacy and the love.

Miss Cornett's Courtship

The Beginning The Courtship

Doubting

The Pain and The Grief

The Wedding

The Courtship

Blue had claimed dominion of the sky, and the small white frame church leaned against its mass in weary resignation. Two tree coated mountains, Pine and Big Black, silently guarded the valley below, ever watchful for some slight transgression of its merely mortal inhabitants. In a nearby meadow, an army of slender green struggled with the breeze for possession of the sun, but ultimately it was the girl's white dress that captured the light. Samuel Patton Caudill noticed it at once, and from that moment on all other battles held no interest for him. He put aside toy soldiers and, for the first time, became a man.

Dora's eyes found his in almost the same instant, and the small smiles and subtle gazes began almost at once. The letters quickly followed; she could never quite remember who started that litany of hastily exchanged notes which eventually progressed to lengthy penned correspondences. Her hesitation in loving him was minute, though she knew from the beginning it would not be an easy thing between them. But Patton had much more to offer than it might appear to the casual observer. Though the innocence of youth still shone bright in his eager eyes, he'd seen war; he'd proven himself to be a man of courage. Beyond that was honesty and a hard work ethic and above all things, she knew without a doubt, a propensity of love for her. It could work, given half a chance. Shy and demure as she was, Dora intended to give it more than that.

June 7, 1904

My dear Miss Dora—

As the kind old rain has stretched forth his tender hand bidding me to discontinue all further labor for today, I will endeavor to respond to your loving call and to return as far as is consistent with me the loving hand and tender heart that was bestowed upon me by the sweet words that composed the little "missive" I found awaiting me upon my return home. "The missive" was read, reread, and read again, trying to find some dissatisfactory expressions, but with all my scrutinizing perusals I am the happy boy to relate to you that the more I read, the more bubbles I could see forming on the lachrymal lakes of those soft eyes, that are at all times smiling at me and reassuring me that just beyond is to be found a treasure of a triple value.

Yours,
P.C.

The church, a curious matchmaker, brought them together — he from his side of the mountain, and she from the green-carpeted Cumberland valley. Patton thanked God often that his father was a Methodist, for only that trek across the hill with his family every Sunday could have given him the opportunity to meet her. Dora Cornett's world was as different from his as the mountains from the valley. She came from a place of advantages, whereas he knew work as the only means of survival. Dora was school-educated, whereas Patton had obtained most of his knowledge from book reading, not that it left him lacking. Besides, none of that mattered. What had books to do with love? And Patton had fallen in love with her in that single second when her dress had seized the light and flung it toward him like angels' wings.

She was an angel, Dora was. Everything about her was heavenly: the golden glints in her wavy brown hair, the heart-shaped curve of her face, her gentle doe- like brown eyes, her soft mouth.... Their first kiss had been short and sweet, barely between hello and goodbye, but how glad he was he had claimed it. That kiss had expressed everything. And seeing beyond her shyness, Patton felt certain Dora's sentiments about him were the same—love-filled and genuine. Some things were like that. You could just tell.

July 5, 1904

To my only Sweet-Heart—

While the low heavy peals of thunder can be so distinctly heard and the tiny raindrops are chasing each other along the eaves, and playing pitter-patter on my window sill, I will make an effort to answer the little missive that presented its sweet face at my cozy little mansion about eight o'clock p.m. this evening.

Honey, you know I would never call you foolish. Now if that is your only excuse for not writing any more than you did, please for my sake say all you want to, for Little Patton could willingly and gladly sit up all night long if he could only have such loving letters as those of Sweet Dora's to peruse.

Oh! Miss Dora, when can I once more be the happy boy to press those ruby lips to mine? Could I only be with you always. How long do you intend keeping me away?

When we are married...we will keep house in the clouds, curtain our windows with sun-tinted mists, with purple vapors hang the couch and pillow it with a white puff of fog. Eh, honey?

Patton

Their courtship had progressed much more rapidly than she'd expected. Soon, he began coming to call, sometimes on Sundays after service, others on some trip across the mountain for this or that. Dora's heart sang at the thought of each meeting, each caressing gaze from him, each casual brush of her hand. Every time together was a precious treasure, to be considered and reflected on with tenderness later, when she was alone. She kept a careful record of their love's progression in her journal. It was one thing for him to be her "friend" though, but Father would never approve of him as more. 'Low-born,' her father would say, and Dora could just hear him now. 'Won't ever come to amount to anything much. Those Caudills have always been poor, poor, poor. Good folk, but common.'

‘But when I look at him,’ she told her diary, ‘I see light, and happiness, and I wish....I wish.’

She tossed the quill aside and stared down at her spidery script. What did she wish, Dora wondered? For the millionth time she picked up the letter and reread it. Patton’s wishes seemed pretty clear. He wanted to kiss her. To hold her. To build ‘cloud houses’ with her.

But Dora knew she wanted more than fairy tales. Some elusive something in Patton would make her more than she was, and she wanted to find that something and give it her life. She sighed and let her gaze stray out her window, her thoughts drifting in and out with the breeze-blown lace curtains.

“But Father would never approve,” she whispered. “Never.”

Then she picked up the quill once more, with determination, and prepared to answer Patton's letter.

The thought that William Wesley Cornett might not approve of him never entered Patton's mind. To him, people were just people, and he and Dora had destiny drawing them together, like night to day. William Cornett's disgruntled looks when Patton came to call on Dora didn't phase him in the least. He assumed the man had a speck of dust in his eye, or an infirmary was in some way paining him. Patton was that naive, and preferred to remain so. He'd seen enough of warring in the Philippines; he had no desire for it to follow him home.

"I'm not sure how Papa feels about your calling, Patton," Dora would say timidly, perhaps trying to warn him, as they sat knees barely touching in the porch swing, sipping lemonade.

Patton's laughter chased away any bad feelings. In his mind, concern had no place with the two of them, an unwelcome intruder to the sweetness of their companionship. "Your Papa likes me, Doe," he'd tell her, ignoring the slightly disbelieving shake of her head. "I can tell. Your Mama, too."

"Oh, Patton," Dora smiled with that angelic smile of hers, "you are so sweet."

Patton stole a tiny kiss just behind her ear. "It's you, my dear. You are the sweet one."

And that was the truth, plain and simple, according to his book.

I try not to worry, Stella," Dora told her friend. "And I don't when he's around. It's impossible to worry when Patton's close by. But when he's gone, I worry all the time. I know Mama would never say a thing, but Papa gives me disapproving eyes. It frightens me."

Stella brushed a crumb of shortbread from her skirt. She had an unparalleled fondness for sweets, one surpassed only by her love for Dora. They'd been friends as long as they could both remember. Even her beau, Charles Smurfield, "Mr. Smusby" as she knew Dora referred to him behind her back, would never come between them.

"What do you think your Papa would do if he knew you were in love with Patton?" she asked.

"Heaven only knows," Dora replied. "I shudder to think."

"But Patton's a nice boy, Dora. You could do worse, I would think."

Dora shrugged. "You know how Papa is. He has this idea about education and bettering oneself and I think he'd like to see me leave the valley."

Shock registered instantly on Stella's face. "Leave!" Stella found it almost impossible to conceive of life beyond the two big mountains she'd known since her birth. She would feel naked out there, she thought with a vague bit of shame. Naked, and lonely.

Dora patted her friend's arm reassuringly. "Calm down, dear. I'd never leave you. Or Patton. It's just what Papa wants, I think."

"What on earth would you do?"

"Oh, teach school, I expect. That's what occupation claims most young ladies. But unfortunately, I have no desire to be a schoolmarm."

Stella yawned, then fanned herself with her flower-papered fan. "It's warm today, isn't it, dear?"

Dora smiled, knowing she'd reached the end of Stella's attention span. She was a darling, but she couldn't handle anything serious for more than five minutes. She and "Smusby" would make quite a pair, for they both loved nothing better than to eat and sleep.

"It is hot, Stell," she replied, realizing she'd be getting no further advice about her problem here. "How about a nap?"

Watson's cough was getting worse. Patton thought guiltily of all the times he'd tried to keep his brother away from Dora, fearing she'd find the tall dark physique of Watson more attractive and eligible. Now he'd give anything to know his brother would be with him forever, laughing with him and Dora, best man at their wedding, counselor for life. Such might not be the case Patton knew, for he'd seen this kind of illness before, a slow killing kind for which there was no known cure.

"Hey, Pat," Watson called out in a husky voice from the other room. "Come and tell me the news from your trip."

Patton ambled to his brother's side, trying to shake off his sense of foreboding, provide what little cheer he could, which he feared wouldn't be much. He and his Cousin Rollin had just returned from a short trip through Knott and Perry counties. They'd gone with a dual purpose—to hunt and to see if they could find any work besides the logging and sharecropping available in Letcher. Luck was not with them, unfortunately. They chased several squirrels and one fat rabbit but weren't able to snare a thing; and no one they met knew of any suitable employment. They returned home with empty hands and empty pockets.

"Not much to tell, brother," Patton said quietly, and hopefully not too dejectedly. He took a seat in the cane backed rocker beside Watson's bed.

"Couldn't chase down any critters or foul; no work to be found neither. Sad state of affairs there as well as here, I'm afraid."

Watson shook his head, another dry cough racking his body. When it subsided, he stroked Patton's arm in consolation. "You'll do all right," he said. "You've a head on your shoulders." He laughed weakly. "Long as you don't let your heart get the better of it."

Patton's gave his brother a now irritated look, as if offering a cautious dare.

“Oh, I know you love her,” Watson grinned, still eager to take up the gauntlet. “But love shouldn’t get in the way of a man making his way. Of duty. And your first duty is to yourself. Don’t take on too much.”

“I’ve done my duty—by my country.” Patton hoped his tone wasn’t too sharp or too harsh. He’d no desire to quarrel with his brother now. But he knew his mind. He would not have it questioned. “In Cuba I had my time for duty. That’s all in the past now. I want time for love.”

“You won’t have time for much love whilst you’re trying to make a living, Pat. Supporting a family in these mountains won’t be an easy task.”

“Then maybe I’ll leave.” Patton intended not to be dissuaded by his brother’s negativity. He had his whole life. The whole world waited for him. For him and his Doe.

Watson looked only slightly surprised at Patton's announcement. He coughed again and wiped his mouth with his already blood-stained handkerchief. "You're God-awful determined, Pat. I'll say that for you."

"I got a reason to be, brother. A damn good reason."

The night owl hooted like a broken bugler, shaking Patton out of a fitful sleep. His body was still damp with sweat; the bedclothes were twisted with his nocturnal battle. He'd been dreaming again. Dreaming about the war. Dreaming about all those who died such terrible deaths. Deaths of disease. Deaths of violent shatterings. Deaths of despair. How many had he seen, he wondered? How had he, so young, so weak, managed to be one of the survivors?

Whoo...whoo... the sound filled up the night, asking the question he so very often asked himself. Who was he to be alive? Who...when so many had died—so young, younger than him even.

Since then, he'd wanted only peace in his life. No more fighting. Coming back to the hills hadn't been easy. Fighting had always seemed to be a way of life here. One clan was always feuding with another. Luckily the Caudills didn't have much of anything anyone wanted. They were poor; they worked and minded their own affairs. But someone was always getting killed in these mountains—over a woman, a horse, sometimes over a few dollars. So much discord in the midst of all this majestic grandeur. How could it be? He wondered God didn't strike them all dead for being so self-absorbed.

Patton reached for his pipe then remembered the smoke bothered his brother when it seeped through the mismatched boards of the walls. Better not. He felt so out of sorts though. Like he'd never sleep again. And every night the same thing. Dreams, then fitful sleeping, then wakefulness.

Only one thing seemed to calm his anxiety. One thing alone could set his churning soul to restfulness. He reached over to the Bible on his bedside table. Inside the heavy leather bound book was a packet of letters, tied up with a short length of twine. Patton pulled the string and the letters spilled onto the bed like eager friends. He picked up the first, dated only a month earlier, and started to read.

The reading went on until the first streaks of dawn sang their morning prelude to the day. By then, Patton was more than ready to face whatever morning, noon or night had to offer. He knew now he would fight for tomorrow if need be. He'd certainly prefer however, to saunter along peaceably, enjoying each moment as it came.

First things first, though. Smiling, Patton reached for his quill and began.

July 11, 1904

Dearest Dora—

Say dear, how many moons must rise and set ere I can claim you as my own and my arms may entwine that supple waist, my eyes look squarely into yours and a love be exchanged between us that will remain unsevered through all eternity.

Please don't call me an impatient little imp for I earnestly can't be quiet until I get full compensation for the heart that some honeysuckle has taken. Believe me, dearest, at this hour my heart is beating at an unlimited speed and that last "I long to see you" a-ringing in my ears.

Love, how near you seem to me today. Please don't look upward but instead, turn your loving eyes this way that I may once more drink from the fountain of bliss that seems so near, but, I fear, is nestled away way off, so doggedly far that I can never, never reach it. What say you, Dora? Am I, or am I not your choice?

Speak, dear. Oh! Should the angel of my life flee from me, I would feel as one eternally doomed. Now I have expressed myself too candidly, but I will not recall a single word until you bid me to do so.

Love,
P.C.

William Wesley Cornett ushered his family into their pew. He tried not to feel prideful as he entered the church every Sunday, but it was difficult. He knew this Methodist gathering was here because of his generosity, just as the town of Poor Fork was here because of his hard work. William had come to the valley thirty years ago, as quite a young man, with his then-small family. Now, their number had grown to fifteen, and the congregation had grown to a modest population of one hundred plus. Some came from as far away as twenty miles, just for services. But it was the Lord who brought them out, he reminded himself, not the fact that William Wesley Cornett would be present.

Of course, he knew there was one here who wasn't drawn by the good Lord—Patton Caudill. Patton Caudill attended for one reason, and one reason alone: William's daughter Dora. He guffawed at the thought of it. Patton Caudill was a nice enough sort, hardworking and honest, but he was poor as a church mouse and only self-educated to boot. William had a better future than Patton could ever hope to offer planned for Dora. His girls had all had education; they could go out in the world, leave this valley, have something more for themselves. It was his dream for his children to have life easier than he had. To work, yes, but not to the extent that it wore them down and made them old before their time. William had watched that happen to Mary Jane; he didn't want it for the girls. So far though, none of them had been wise enough to take their chance. One by one, each had married and gone to homes scattered across the hills and valleys. One by one they grew old while still in the midst of their youth. But Dora still had a chance. Dora was his last hope.

He looked over at his wife now, remembering when she had been young Mary Jane Kelly, bright and beautiful and gay. His success hadn't come soon enough to save her. Now she had little life left, after all the children and all the hard work. Mary Jane was tough, and she'd given her all, but it had left her with lifeless eyes and a sad countenance. Now William had to watch as it happened to his girls. With husbands like Patton Caudill, whose family had practically given their land away for coal and lumber money. Now, they had nothing left. Nothing to offer any woman but a life of hard work. Dora deserved better.

The congregation rose to sing the first hymn and he tried to get his mind back on godly thoughts. Out of the corner of his eyes he could see Patton, eyeing his daughter every few seconds, and Dora's sheltered glances back at him over her hymnal. Damn...how was he going to keep these two apart? He knew any efforts to dissuade the romance would only result in their determination to continue it. But there must be some way, something he could do to make Dora see the importance of her education. Of leaving Poor Fork.

He caught her eye and gave her his sternest look. Dora's gaze fell to the book in hand, sufficiently chastened. For now, that would do. But what about later, he wondered?

Patton tiptoed around the side of the building and grabbed Dora from behind, tickling her ribs until she giggled out loud. How he did love to hear the sweet melody of her laughter!

"Patton! Stop it!" She immediately lowered her voice to a whisper and looked around as if expecting someone to discipline her for misbehavior.

Patton ignored her concern and kissed her smack on her rosy lips.

"Patton! Don't! Papa will see us."

He laughed out loud. "What do I care? What do I care if the whole world sees us? I love you, Doe. I'm going to marry you, just as soon as school's over this fall!"

"And how do you know Papa will be agreeable to that?" she asked.

The sweet taste of her kiss still on his lips gave him courage. "I don't care if he isn't agreeable. You'll run away with me, won't you?"

Dora shook her head, and he wondered if that meant yes, no, or maybe. Patton wasn't always too sure about Dora's womanly thoughts. Sometimes she seemed so reserved and distant; others so warm he scarcely dared dream what really loving her might be like.

"Wouldn't you, dearest? Please say you would. Don't break poor Patton's heart."

She took a step back from him as if some unseen force was propelling her backward. The force quickly became known, however. "Mr. Caudill, I hardly think you should be calling me dearest. Tisn't appropriate."

Patton saw that her eyes had gone beyond him, and he turned to find Dora's father standing there with a stern expression. "Dora, we're leaving now."

"Yes, Papa."

Mr. Cornett acknowledged Patton with a curt nod. "Good day, Caudill."

"Good day, Mr. Cornett." He watched Dora follow her father obediently, without even a backward glance his way. At times like this, he wondered if she really did love him. If she really would follow him to the ends of the earth as she'd said in her letters. He laughed. Of course Dora would follow him, he decided. Why on earth wouldn't she? He planned to conquer the world for her.

July 21, 1904

Dearest—

I have every one of your letters to me spread out on the table before me. Now if I only had my own darling Dora near by where I could place my arm around her supple waist and put 3 successive kisses right squarely in the same sweet spot I put the last one, it would require the strength of two of the best horses in Letcher to pull me loose from you.

By the way, did you get home safely Sunday? My folks at home says to me just as soon as I was in talking distance, "Why do you get back so early? We know she has thrown you and taken another fellow."

Guess I will attend a social at Mr. McClure's on Saturday night. If it would not inconvenience you too much, please be up at that time and if it pleases you I will return home with you.

Begging you to excuse all imperfections and hoping a hasty reply

I subscribe voraciously,
P.C.

Dora admired her friend Stella's golden curls; she would make a pretty picture at the social tonight. Glancing in the mirror briefly, she wondered what exactly Patton Caudill found to love in her own face. She thought she always looked a little sad, though she never really felt that way, the lines just seemed to be etched into her face, perhaps a memory of sadness buried in some long past ancestral sorrow. Dora had a feeling her ancestors had know many sorrows; she'd seen them outlined in her mother's face too. Oh well, she sighed, such must be the lot of the Kelly stock. Better to accept than anguish about it.

Tonight she would have good reason to smile and bring some light to that sad expression. She was a bit surprised Papa was allowing her to go to this social. She knew how much he disliked Patton. Not disliked, really, just disapproved. She'd expected him to be more indignant about their courting, but he just remained silent, not a word of criticism passing his lips. Just the looks, that was all. Looks were enough to keep her guilt intact though.

"Come on Doe. We'll be late." Stella cut into her thoughts like a pouting child, obviously growing impatient to be with her Mr. Smusby.

Life would be simple for them, Dora imagined. They'd jig dance at their wedding, have a passel of children, and live contentedly if not happily ever after. Somehow, Dora did not think her own way would be so simple. But all these worries were for another day.

Tonight, she and Patton would laugh and dance their cares away. And maybe, just maybe, he would kiss her again. His kisses gave her tingles where tingles shouldn't be.

“I’m ready,” she said with a secretive smile and, linking her arm in her friend’s, turned toward the door.

A school of familiar faces swam around Patton like so many fish in a pond. Would she never get here? It seemed he’d been waiting all evening and still not sign of her. Nothing mattered to him anymore except her. Not work, not play, not even drinking, though his brothers often encouraged him to come out to the still with them for a swig. No, that was all in the past for Patton. He wanted only to sit and daydream of Dora, of their future together, their cloud castles.

“How are you, Patton?” a seductive feminine voice whispered in his ear. Cousin Polly.

An army of thoughts invaded his mind as he slowly turned his eyes toward her. It had been a long time, hadn't it? Before the war. Before he'd fallen in love with Dora.

Polly stood there, pretty as ever with her rosy cheeks and dark curls. "Can I give you a kiss?" A little laugh escaped her at their old joke, and she pressed a foil-wrapped chocolate into his hand. Her touch alarmed him a little. Still warm. Too warm, he thought; or was that merely the flush he felt creeping into his own cheeks?

"How are you, Polly?"

"I'm just fine, Patton. And you? I haven't seen much of you since you got back from the fighting."

A twinge of guilt invaded him.

"I've missed you."

What could he say? What should he say? "Polly, I...."

Before he could utter another word,

the room seemed to light up. Could her white dress really put forth such an intense glow? Or was it more than that, something deep inside her that shone out like a candle lighting a foggy holler? Everything suddenly slowed and stood still and Patton felt absolutely positive that he needn't say another word to his cousin; understanding had dawned painfully on her face.

She faded into the fog with the rest of them, leaving him abruptly and without shame at Dora's side, little more than a lovestruck schoolboy.

A dance, then another, and then still another. Dora had no idea whether or not she was breathless from all the dancing, or simply from desire. The way the palm of his hand pressed gently into the small of her back, the way her head just fit into the crook of his shoulder, the way he smelled of tobacco and fresh air —she felt such a need to be close, closer, to him than she'd ever experienced in her life. She supposed it was love, but in her practical way wondered if perhaps it might be nothing more than her tight corset and all the exertion.

"Do you love me, Miss Cornett?" He whispered it so slightly that she had to strain to catch the words. Had he been reading her mind?

"That is a rather personal question, isn't it, Mr. Caudill?" she teased.

He laughed and stopped in the middle of the dance floor. Dora knew everyone was looking at them now and she felt the rush of blood coloring her face. She hated to be the center of attention, hated to think people were watching her. Patton, of course, was just the opposite. "Please..." she whispered.

"Please, what?" he teased back.

"Please...can we dance?"

"Is that what you really want to do? Just dance."

Dora knew she would have no peace unless she gave him the answer he sought. So like a man, she thought, but even in the midst of her irritation in crept the tingle she so often experienced in his presence.

"No...not really," she said, just loud enough for him to hear.

Patton squeezed her waist and led her toward the door. A million eyes followed them, she felt certain, but only one set of them caught her attention—the eyes of Polly Caudill, eyes angry enough to burn down houses. Or kill. Dora wondered why such hate-filled eyes were staring at her.

August 3, 1904

My Own Darling,

It was all I could do to prevent myself from seizing hold of you when you came into the room last night.

Dearest, how could you even think me to be a flatterer? You were sadly mistaken in your presumptions. If there is any thing in the world I would detest, it is a "flattery genius." I was sincere in every word I said to you.

I think of you so often that you have become a part of my life. Reason and please, for my sake—never let the thought enter your mind that I am or could possibly be a naughty flatterer. I am desirous to be granted the privilege of an extended tete a tete with you. Now if you are not too busy after school hours tomorrow, or just any time complying with your wishes. Please let me know.

All my love,
Patton

Doubting

Dora watched her mother tirelessly kneading bread, two grandchildren playing a game of catch-me-if-you- can around her skirts. Mary Jane Cornett's back arched over her task and her faded cotton dress and stray wisps of graying hair reminded Dora that her mother had led a difficult life, coming to these mountains in her youth, having it stripped from her like veneer from quality wood. Mary Jane had been a minister's daughter, raised in a good Virginia home, where she had comfort and pretty things. She must have loved Dora's father very much to give everything up for him. And what had it gotten her, except old before her time?

For the first time, Dora thought perhaps she understood her father's reluctance for her to marry Patton. There would be work, and babies, and more work, and more babies. Is this what she would be like in twenty years? Maybe even ten?

Her mother's gentle brown eyes met hers over the table in some kind of tacit understanding. "Doe?"

"Yes, Ma?"

"Could you pass me that pan behind you on the stove?"

She handed the heavy iron backing dish to her mother, recognizing the toll even such a small task as bread-making took on a woman. Then, there was washing, cooking, mending, gardening—all this and children, and then whatever else needed attention during the day.

"You seem a million miles away, girl," her mother remarked, smiling.

Dora laughed lightly. "Actually," she said slowly, "I'm right here." She paused, wondering if it would really be wise to bring up the subject. Would her mother encourage, or dissuade? Which would she rather hear?

"Ma..." she hesitated, as her mother raised those weary eyes to meet hers. "Ma, you and Pa...are you sorry you married him? Came away from Virginia with him?"

Instantly, her mother's mouth bent in a bittersweet smile filled with misty memories. "Oh, Dora...the things you ask."

For a moment she thought perhaps that was the only comment her mother was going to make. The two boys playing under the table popped their heads out and chanted, "Grandma loves Grandpa, Grandma loves Grandpa."

"Shoo, you boys," Mary Jane told them. "Enough of you. Out of my kitchen now."

They scampered away like mice, each grabbing a horse apple from the fruit bowl on their way out. Children, Dora thought. Their making was another matter to be considered. She blushed at the thought of it.

Mary Jane brushed the flour from her hands and came around the table to sit next to her daughter. "You day-dreaming, Doe? Wondering what your future holds? Who your prince will be?"

"I guess I am a little." Dora squeezed her mother's hand. "I guess I'm wondering if princes and happy endings exist."

Her mother shook her head sadly. "I'm afraid they don't, my love. Not really. Duty exists, and love exists. Sometimes they co-exist. But happy endings are just in fairy tales."

"You're not happy, then? Were you ever happy?"

Mary Jane sighed, eyes moist. "Oh, yes, daughter, I was happy. I remember the idyllic days of courting and first passion. But passion fades and leaves the rest."

Dora felt fear welling up in her breast, suffocating her joy. "What is the rest then? Is there no hope?"

"You must find your own way, Dora. I've learned enough not to try and tell you this or that, though your Pa would have me try. I can't say the love you take won't be worth whatever work or suffering may come your way. Would I trade mine? I don't know. I still love your Pa. But it's been hard. I turned my back on my own family to go with him. In some ways I never forgave myself." She paused, surely remembering some long gone drama of her own. "I guess the best advice I can give you, daughter, is to make your own decision and never look back. Keep moving forward no matter what happens. No matter what you may regret. A choice must always be made at the expense of another. That's the way of life."

Her mother rose and went back to the bread, kneading it with sudden and renewed vigor. Dora knew the conversation was over. Her mother was not a woman of many words, and already she'd given much more than Dora would have expected.

Dora turned to leave the room, knowing she had lessons to prepare for the next day. Then, her mother spoke once more. "You could ask Patton to take my cow to sell? It would be a help."

Dora nodded. Such was her mother's way of saying Patton was a welcome visitor, at least as far as she was concerned.

Well I think she's gone beyond the pale," Stella told Dora as they bounced to and fro in the back of the wagon on the road to school. "Who does she think she is, spreading rumors like that? Have you spoken to Patton about it?"

"No, Stella. I trust Patton. He would have told me if there was something between him and Polly Caudill."

Stella pursed her mouth obstinately. "Dora, you shouldn't trust a man that much. I don't even trust Charles that much. Besides, if it's not true, then why was Polly telling everyone at the social that Patton had as much as promised to marry her before he went off to fight?"

"Maybe she just wanted him to, Stell. Maybe it's what she hoped."

Dora wished Stella would drop the subject, because every time she thought of it she felt very uncomfortable. What if Patton really had made promises to Polly? Wouldn't it be his responsibility to keep them? And then where would that leave her? Alone? Was that what she wanted?

"And you know what else, Doe," Stella continued, "Yesterday I saw her heading out toward Letcher with a picnic basket. Now where do you think she was going with that?"

Dora was becoming visibly irritated. "Oh Stella, I'm sure I don't know. Neither do I care to speculate. Could we drop this subject now? Please?"

Stella looked a little hurt but shut her mouth with a snap. The sharp cry of a jay filled the air, echoing

Dora's own pain. She remembered the tenderness of Patton's lips against hers the night of the social; the way his hand had pressed against her back when he'd held her, kissed her. Patton had said he would never hurt her. That he loved her beyond all love. Surely, he wouldn't withhold the truth about something as serious as that. Would he?

Patton watched his brother outside in the distance. Watson seemed better today, and Cousin Polly had brought over a picnic lunch and suggested they sit near the big oak tree on the hill and eat. His brother lay stretched out like a sunning cat on a faded cotton quilt, laughing at something she's said, happiness evident on his pale face.

Patton, however, questioned Polly's motives. When he and Dora had come inside after their brief “interlude” at the social, he’d seen Polly flirting shamelessly with every man with whom she came in contact. Then suddenly, after months of staying away from the Caudill place entirely, she’d been to see Watson three times in the past two weeks. Watson, not Patton. She’d made it very clear she had no desire to speak to him whatsoever. But why, he wondered, was she suddenly pursuing Watson, whom she’d shown no interest in before? The ways of women--even Dora whom he adored--so often baffled him. But he had a niggling suspicion about Polly’s sudden interest.

His brother seemed delighted with the attention though. Watson, in his healthier days, had had quite an interest in the ladies. They’d had quite an interest in him, too, so it was something of an irony that Cousin Polly had always favored Patton. He knew she had too; her not so subtle caresses and flirtation had told him so, though he'd never encouraged her beyond a couple of quick kisses behind the barn. Whatever she imagined he had promised, it was all in her head. Those days, Patton had little care for anything except the war; only since returning had he turned his whole mind toward loving Dora. Why did Polly have to reappear in his life now?

Again, he looked across the wide expanse of green toward his brother. Watson's deteriorating condition had slowed his wild ways down a good bit, and Patton knew he must be glad of someone once more showing attentiveness. Why did that someone have to be Polly Caudill, though? Patton had a bad feeling about it, and despite the sunshine and the birdsong and his love for Doe, he couldn't seem to shake off the premonition that it would only lead to pain.

Why did the children seem rowdier than usual today? Dora wondered. Were they really, or was it just her imagination, fueled by her recent conversation with her mother? Mary Jane hadn't given Dora much hope for a happy ending.

While Stella guided the younger children with their numbers, Dora took pause from her grading to study her situation. This was her last session at school. She and Stella were teachers-in-training now. After December, she could go home and take care of Ma and Pa, or marry and take care of Patton, or leave the valley to teach, thereby taking care of a whole passel of youngsters who weren't even her own. What choices, she thought without much hope for happiness, even though she knew Patton would bring her love.

She turned her gaze out to the window. In the distance loomed the two mountains which had always been in her sight. Just beyond Big Black were Ma and Pa and the rest of her family, scattered out like sheep across the hills and hollers. There lay loyalty and duty. Had love and romance no place in her life at all?

The boys had their way laid out. They were given their land, and they farmed it or found trades, or helped Pa with the store. And her sisters...most had chosen to marry. Then they'd moved away from home and, for the most part, begun their sad lives of decline. But Pa had given them all the chance for more. They had all gone to school, and been trained to teach if they'd had the desire. She knew she was Pa's last hope. She was the last daughter smart enough, tough enough, to leave and make a strong life for herself beyond Appalachia. Dora knew what was in her father's mind. And the call to obey was strong.

Her thoughts were interrupted by the clanging of the school bell, announcing the end of another day. She watched the children quickly scatter out of the room, wishing her direction in life could be decided as simply, by the mere ringing of a bell.

Stella, apparently talked out for the time being, started gathering up her materials and clearing the blackboard. Once again, Dora's eyes found the mountains. But this time, it was Pine Mountain that held her gaze. Pine, further in the distance but just as grand. Pine, beyond which Patton made his home, the home he would also make with Dora. She thought of his love, his loyalty, his desire to share his life with her. A single shaft of light struck something shiny at the peak of the mountain, reminding her that for every person's plan there is a greater plan.

"What is the plan for me?" she whispered. "For me?" Then she said a silent prayer that God did indeed know best, and would guide her toward peace, and the right place.

I haven't the slightest idea what you mean, Patton," Polly replied shrilly to his remark. "As you yourself said, what we had together is all in the past."

Patton tried to keep his irritation in hand. "We had nothing together, Pol, and you know it."

She bit her lip, looking wounded. "I'd say your kisses proved otherwise," she insisted softly.

"Polly, a kiss is a kiss. You knew I was off to fight. You knew the chances were pretty good I'd never come back. How could I have promised you anything?"

Polly made a fuss of typing her bonnet strings, apparently unbothered by his remark. “Well, it’s all water under the bridge now, isn’t it? Now it’s me and Watson. So you needn’t trouble yourself at all.”

She made to leave, but he grabbed her arm to hold her in place. “What do you mean it’s you and Watson?’ Watson is not a well man, Polly. He won’t be having intentions towards anyone, if that’s what you’re thinking.”

Polly smiled smugly, as if she knew a secret she wasn’t about to share. “Maybe he’s not so sick as you think he is, little brother. And I do hope you aren’t jealous.”

Patton found his voice had gone completely, and he could do little more than stare at her, open-mouthed. What exactly was she implying? he wondered.

Before he had time to ponder further though, Polly had her basket in hand and was heading for her buggy. “We’ll be one big happy family, won’t we, Patton? Me, Watson, and you and Dora Cornett.” She laughed as she climbed into her rig. He didn’t like the sound of it. Not one bit.

“One big happy family,” Polly said again. And with that, she clucked at her horse and directed the buggy into the distant twilight.

August 7, 1904

Dearest—

I don't think I am a deceitful man.

As I told you in a preceding letter, "if the angel of my life (that is Dora) should fly from me my castle would fall never to be rebuilt again."

There has been an inclusive longing for you in my heart since our first meeting. I did not know what love meant until I got acquainted with you. I love you so devotedly that there isn't any pinnacle so high, or depression so low, but what I would fling from or dive into—in order to save my "blushing little Dora."

I promise I will try to be less troublesome henceforth. Please excuse such imperfections and reckless blunders.

I remain,
affectionately your lover...

It had been too long since he'd held her, Patton thought as he watched Dora coming down the stairs and out the porch door. He wanted to hold her so badly now he could almost feel her supple waist in his arms and smell the sweet clovery scent of her. But Mr. Cornett was in the parlor, watching like a sheep dog for some sign of misbehavior.

"Hello, Patton," she said quietly as she let the screen door close gently behind her.

"I've missed you," he whispered. "I wish you'd let me come sooner."

She shrugged, noncommital. "I've been quite busy. You know, school, and things..." Her voice strayed away but he thought he heard a note of hesitation before it was gone.

Patton knew she was troubled. Troubled by gossip and speculation. Her last letter had implied as much. She'd spoken of her uncertainty, her lack of faith. What could he say to make her believe? Words meant so little, really.

"Could we walk a little?" he asked shyly. Suddenly he felt like a schoolboy in her presence, so much did he want her love and laughter to touch him again.

Within moments they were heading down the dusty road, her father's, "Don't you stray too far, Dora," ringing in their ears.

"Doe..." he stopped, completely at a loss. Would she not help him at all?

Her silence told him she would not. "There is no truth to it. None."

Finally, she spoke, not slowing her pace or

looking at him. “Why is she there, Patton? I hear she is at your place often. Why?”

“She’s courting Watson.”

That caused her to laugh, but it wasn’t a laugh he enjoyed. It was a laugh filled with sarcasm, something he’d never known Dora possessed. He still had much to learn about her, it appeared.

“Watson?” She sighed. “Poor Watson.”

“I think she’d like for me to be jealous of them. But I’m not Doe. I swear I’m not.”

This time she did stop. She stopped and faced him and her eyes met his like the eyes of judge and jury. “What was she to you, Patton? What? Did you write the same sweet letters to her that now you write to me?”

Shock racked him. How could she think such a thing? How?

He took her by both arms and met her gaze directly. The sun was just beginning to set and the sky was cast with a peach haze that looked so sweet you almost wanted to eat it up. She had to believe him. He had to make her believe him. When he spoke to her, his voice resonated with a truth so pure and so true it almost seemed like God himself talking.

"No, I never wrote her. Never. She was nothing. She flirted with me before the war; she even kissed me and for just a moment, I suppose I did kiss her back. But she was nothing to me. I never thought of her while I was gone. Never. And ever since I've known you, Doe, there has been no other, nor ever will be. You are my light...and my life. I want our hearts to be joined together with a golden seal to hold fast through endless eternity."

Dora must have seen the light glowing in his eyes and it must have touched her. Because she turned her face upward, upward to meet his, and right there before God and her father's house returned his kiss with one so passionate and filled with love that Patton knew they would never doubt one another again. They had come home to one another.

Yes, Dora thought, this was what she wanted. Patton was her home. She knew it wouldn't be easy. Life never was, she supposed, but something in Patton's declaration, something pure and true and straight from the heart of the angels touched her and she knew her destiny lay with him. Whatever life might bring, it would bring it to them together, so she could imagine no life without him. Pa would have to be convinced, but her sisters had done it, and so could she. Time had come to stop debating and begin. Time had come.

But no sooner had she thought it than the black horse, kicking up a trail of dust behind it, came flying down the lane bringing with it a storm of bitter tears that would make Dora pause to doubt love's outcome once again.

The Pain and The Grief

They huddled like forlorn children around the small open grave, silent and without hope. Not even God could bring back what was taken.

Dora looked over the tiny wooden casket at her sister Sudie, dark-eyed and emotionless. Had Sudie's tears all been shed, leaving only the empty shell of a young mother behind? How, Dora wondered, could one bear to lose a child? So small, so helpless? What was the point of finding love if it resulted in grief like this?

She brushed a drop of rain from her face. Rain, or tears? At least God had the decency to cry, too, she thought. Of course God would cry at their loss. It was hard to understand but maybe some things were better left without explanation. If people knew too much, perhaps they wouldn't be faithful.

Patton's bent head caught her glance. She'd told him not to come, not today, but he'd said nothing would keep him away; his place was near her and her loss. Oh Patton, she thought, couldn't you just leave me to my grief for one day?

From the moment the black horse had flown up the lane, and she'd learned that Sudie's little George had died of measles, her doubt had latched onto her once more. For a single instant her love for Patton had triumphed, and she'd truly thought herself safe from fear, but, all-too-quickly, it had come flying back with that cloud of dust and heartache. She wanted time alone, to think and think and think some more. To decide if she could bear to risk such as this.

Now, there was pain to think about. Pain, and grief. Life without a loved one. She didn't want Patton to think her heartless, or finicky, but she wouldn't be rushed or pressured. Her life lay ahead of her. Most of it. It wouldn't do to give it away without serious consideration. Her happiness depended on careful thought.

Patton would just have to wait.

Is this what you want, girl? Is it?" Her father's eyes ached, but his words were hard and unfeeling.

"No, Papa," she replied truthfully. Dora knew she did not want pain such as this. She did not want grief or loss. She wanted happiness.

She could see her mother through the kitchen door with Sudie and her other sisters, doing women's things, caressing and supporting. Why wasn't she in there? she wondered. Why was she in here with Papa, talking about the future?

"What else do you think you'll have if you marry, Dora?"

Her father's voice had dropped somewhat, as if he were afraid the sisters, the loving sisters in the other room, might hear.

"I don't know, Papa."

"I only want your happiness, daughter. I only want you to have what they don't."

He nodded his head toward the kitchen, and she studied the scene and wondered if Ma and Sudie and Precious and Malinda and Zerah and Ida knew what they didn't have. Had he given each of them this same sermon before their marriages?

She sighed. "I want my happiness too. How can you be so sure I won't find it with Patton?" She looked hopeful. "Maybe I'll work and be married."

William huffed. “You’re the first that’s had that thought, I’ll give you that.”

Dora realized suddenly how helpless her father looked, sitting there in his big chair with his snow-white hair and lined face. He’d never been a large man, but his grief made him seem smaller somehow, as if the world had dealt him a blow from which he couldn’t stand. He really did care about her. He really did want what was best.

“I’m still thinking on it, Papa. I promise I am. I haven’t given up the thought of leaving...of going away to teach. Sometimes, marriage frightens me too. I don’t want a loss like Sudie’s.”

His eyes met hers, questioning her honesty. When he found it there he nodded, seemingly satisfied for the moment.

“I guess that’s all I can ask, then, isn’t it? That you think on it.”

“I owe you that, Papa,” she said, going to him and placing a light kiss at the top of his forehead. “I owe you, but I freely give it to you, too. Because I love you.”

William smiled and squeezed her hand. “I love you, too, daughter. I love you, too.”

August 13, 1904

My Darling One-

This sad and dreary evening while I feel so lonely, grieving almost to extremes over not getting any reply to my last letter, I pen these few lines to relieve my troubled mind even though they should find themselves among the contents of the wastebasket upon reaching their destination. This week has been a living death.

It has been said that the world is due every man a time of his own. Now it lies in your power to set the day for me to collect my debt. Please make it soon, dearest.

P.C.

The week had been a living hell. Every day that passed without word from her was another day of agony. When would it end? When would she let him come into her life again?

Patton raised the ax and brought it down with a vengeance on the log in front of him. He didn't often get riled to anger, but he was angry now. What had he done? Nothing. Nothing. Given her all the love a man could give. Never loved another. Ever.

Yet still she turned her heart away from him as if it were a lifeless piece of coal from the hills themselves. How much longer could her torture of him continue?

At just that instant, Watson appeared around the corner of the house with his arm around Polly. "Hey, brother!" he hollered, flushed with a red delight

Patton hadn't seen in him for a long time. Polly was making his brother better, that seemed certain. But for how long?

Polly lowered her eyes as they approached. Guilt, perhaps?

Patton nodded silently, unwilling to give in to pleasant conversation with the two of them. They could just take their talking elsewhere, he thought.

Watson, undeterred by his icy behavior, let go of Polly just long enough to slap Patton on the back. "You've been sullen long enough, Pat. Come along to the caves with us."

Yes, Patton thought, that's just what he wanted to do, spend a day with Watson and Polly. Besides, it surprised him Watson even felt up to it; the caves were damp and strenuous.

His eyes must have registered his surprise, for Watson assured him, “I’m well, better than I’ve been in ages. Come, brother, go with us.”

Surprisingly, Polly spoke. “We could ask Dora to go, too, Watson.”

“Of course, we’ll stop for her on the way, Pat.”

Patton was angry for a moment, angry at Polly for making such a stupid suggestion when all she had in mind was troublesome antics. He almost protested. Almost.

But then a little voice said, why not? They should stop for Dora. They would stop for her, and if she didn’t want to accompany them, well, by golly she could watch him head off into the distance with Watson and Polly, and think him happily spending the day in their company. It was a grand idea.

So to Watson and Polly's great dismay, Patton laid down his ax and replied, "Fine and dandy, let's make a day of it!"

"You go on, Dora, go with them."

Dora stared at her mother in disbelief. Of all the times to decide to support her daughter's wish to be with Patton, why pick now? Now, when the last thing Dora wanted was to spend the day with Watson and Polly. She wasn't even sure she wanted to spend it with Patton, under those circumstances.

Still, she had missed him dreadfully. She'd known she was going to have to answer his letters sooner or later, but she just wasn't ready yet. Answering meant things must move ahead. Dora still didn't know if she was ready for that. Despite her love for him, she wanted life to protect her somehow from all the pain and grief she'd witnessed lately. Somehow, she knew she had that protection only here at home. Once away, what would hold it all at bay? She would be a helpless victim to life's tide. Like her sister Sudie, who'd been staying here since little Georgie died, as if this childhood home provided safety for her as well.

"Do come, Dora," Polly said with sickly sweetness, pressing for an answer.

The two men remained silent, watchful for her decision.

"It would be so good to have another woman along," Polly went on. "So nice."

Dora cringed inwardly. If she didn't go, Patton would be with Polly all day long. She didn't want that, either. God, tell me what to do, she prayed.

Almost instantly, it seemed, her prayers were answered—God could be funny like that sometimes. Riding up the lane—in a wagon for the trip, no less—were Stella and Smusby, the perfect companions for an afternoon picnic to Mammouth Cave.

The caves always held a strange fascination for Dora. Terrified of them on the one hand, she nonetheless found herself drawn there time and time again. The trip usually required some planning, for it was quite a long ride across the hills. Dora had been surprised at Patton and his brother's spontaneous appearance. They would be late getting home; she was surprised her mother had agreed to let her go and thought it for the better that her father was away, for he would never have approved of such an outing, especially with Patton.

They sat side by side in the back of Smusby's wagon now, across from Polly and Watson, who seemed quite caught up in each other. Could Polly's behavior really be nothing more than a ploy to get Patton's attention? Dora found it hard to believe—though Polly kept her fingers firmly laced in Watson's, and her gaze never strayed from his face for more than a moment or two. She appeared in all ways smitten. And, Dora thought, Watson seemed much more the person he'd been before the war, lively and flirtatious and gay. It was wonderful to see him so!

"What are you thinking, Doe?" Patton asked her quietly.

"I was thinking your brother looks happy."

Patton looked long and hard at the man across from him. "That he does," he said at last. "I hope it's true."

Dora nodded in agreement. She didn't know Polly Caudill well, and could scarcely imagine a woman playing such a game as to fake at love, but she knew some women did, and hoped this was not the case now.

"I've missed you, Doe."

She turned now, knowing Patton wanted words of love from her. What could she tell him of the doubts in her mind? How could she explain the fear of loving that crept into her bed every night, and stayed her hand when she moved toward the quill to write to him?

"I've missed you, too," she said at last.

He laughed a little bitterly. Bitterness? Had she brought him to that? The sweet carefree Patton...

"I wouldn't have known it."

"Oh, Patton," she sighed, "I wish I could make you understand."

"Understand what?" He spoke in a whisper, but there was an urgency to his tone. "That you don't love me anymore?"

"It isn't that."

"Then what?"

She took a deep breath. "I'm afraid."

He grasped her arm tightly, almost too tightly.

"Of what? I'm here. I'll never let anything hurt you."

"And how will you keep death away, Patton?

How will you protect me from life itself? From growing old before my time?"

Shock rendered him speechless at these words, as if he couldn't believe these words—simple words, nothing he could fight—were keeping her from him.

They reached their destination before Patton had a chance to answer her question. But, she wondered, if he would—or could—have answered it anyway.

The 200-foot drop down in the wooden bucket, into that fathomless black hole, was the worst of it. Even after you'd done it the first time, you still always had the sense of not knowing what lay ahead, the hazards that might befall you in an instant. Dora shivered. Like life, it was. Like her and Patton.

Stella had last minute jitters, as always, and she and her beau decided to remain above ground. Dora supposed they were the type who would always play it safe, choosing to remain on firm land rather than risking dangers—invisible or otherwise.

The men had gone into the blackness first, one at a time; then Polly, squealing like a frightened child.

Dora didn't scream. For her, it wasn't that kind of fear. It was a paralyzing fear, and it made her silent.

When she reached the bottom at last, it wasn't so bad. Once down in the gigantic cavern, the men had lanterns ready and waiting. Dora could never forget that first moment they lit them, when the dark vault became a fairyland instead of a mausoleum. Always...always, it took her breath away.

Gigantic slivers of what looked like ice graced the walls, ceiling, and even the floor of the cave. They grew up and down, sometimes dainty and delicate, others majestically awesome. The shapes shimmered as they caught the candlelight and danced with flickering shadows. She always thought of Christmas here, this wonderland of beauty, asking nothing more than to be adored by its passersby. Dora always gave the adoration.

“Come on, Dora Caudill,” Polly chirped into her reverie. “Are you gonna stand there gawking all day?”

Patton slipped his arm about her waist and they began a slow descent down the slick path, stopping periodically to marvel at the sights. Polly and Watson stayed somewhat behind, giving Watson an easy pace, so for the first time in weeks, Dora and Patton were alone. She sensed his desire to talk, but felt him at a loss for words all the same. She should help him she knew, but right now she really wanted nothing more than to meander along and gaze at the crystal delight around her.

Funny, how you could find meaning in the oddest moments. Reality and fantasy were merging within her, vying for a balance she knew she could never have found above ground. It was all here though, her fear and her desire, somehow managing to co-exist.

“Doe...” Patton’s voice was pleading, and she knew what he wanted to say and really didn’t need his words at all.

She stopped and slipped her hand into his. The tender motion caught him off-guard and she believed, amazingly, his eyes were misty. How like Patton to cry, to shed quiet desperate tears. For her. And how, she asked herself, could I have hurt him so?

Her thoughts were suddenly interrupted by a shriek from Polly. Turning quickly, in the same instant they saw the woman sliding toward them, out of control.

“Polly!” Watson called out, terror in his voice.

Polly grabbed at the slick wall of the cavern, trying to get a grip and stop her descent. But the movement only caused her feet to slip further our from under her, until she was almost rolling. She slammed into Patton’s body, causing him to drop his lantern and pitch them all into complete darkness. Dora held tight to the wooden railing, trying to keep from falling herself and to help Patton keep his balance.

Quicker than she could blink however, Polly lay still and Patton, without warning, lost his footing and tumbled over the edge of the precipice, into the darkness below.

Dora's heart went cold.

It seemed like forever before they heard him move and even knew he was alive. During those long terrible moments, Dora realized what her hesitation in allowing their love might mean. Now, she may very well have lost him entirely. Lost him to a dark and damp death, leaving her to a life without love or any of the other things she feared so very much. Her fear may have cost her a life filled with love.

But Patton did move at last. He was down there, alive. Thank God.

“Pat, are you all right?” Watson called down to him, after appropriately checking Polly’s condition.

“I’m all right, brother,” he replied a little shakily, or so Dora thought.

“I slid more than fell. I’m about twenty feet down. With some rope, I think I’ll be able to make it up without too much trouble.”

“Patton, I’m so sorry,” Polly said, her own fear evident in her voice. “I didn’t mean...”

“I know, Polly. It’s okay. Doe, are you all right there?”

“Yes,” she said simply, knowing she would not be all right until he was back on solid ground and she could hold him in her arms and tell him she loved him and would marry him as soon as they were out of this place and back in the sunlight. That's what she would tell him, and this time nothing—nothing—- was going to change her mind.

Patton's heart soared as he thought back over his afternoon with Dora. When he'd first come around to consciousness, down on that ledge in the cavern, he'd thought only of Dora and her fears, one of them now nearly realized—losing him. Perhaps, he'd thought, she was right; loss of love was too frightening to risk. Maybe he should let her go; let her have her peace of mind. He sighed, thinking how close he'd come to making her fears a reality.

But then he was back on the solid ground of the cavern, and she was throwing her arms around him and clinging for dear life. He'd never known her to show such emotion, and despite the pain in his side, he felt ecstatic. He knew what this meant—it meant love—for life. Forever.

During the ride home she never let his hand go for even an instant. They'd all remained pretty much silent, even Stella and her beau on the wagon seat. It had been an exhausting day for everyone, but for Patton especially. He thought he might have cracked a rib in the fall, but it barely troubled him, so happy was he now. He knew it was only a matter of time before the joyous deed was done and Dora was his forever. If it took a broken rib to bring him such joy, he'd gladly break as many as he had.

He leaned back in the wicker rocker, glad for the comfort of home despite his missing Doe. Watson and Polly were still by her buggy, where they'd been for some time now, and they seemed to him to be having some type of disagreement. In fact, now that he turned his mind to it, Watson's disposition on the trip home seemed much gloomier than before. Had something happened, he wondered, to upset his brother? Did it have something to do with Polly? There, she was in her buggy and going now. She slapped at her horse sharply and never looked back. Something was surely wrong.

Watson's posture as he approached the porch was slumped and slow. For the first time in days, he looked like an old man, the life sapped from him leaving only an empty hull.

"Brother?" Patton called out, the question evident in his voice.

Watson raised his hand, fending his query off, but Patton intended to have none of that. Watson was clearly in pain. Physical or emotional?

"What is it, Wats?"

Watson never made it up the steps, he fell against the post and leaned there, as if any further movement was too much effort to be attempted. Patton was beside him in a second, grabbing his waist despite the pain to his ribs, and helping his brother up to the chair on the porch.

“Was today too much?”

Watson laughed a quiet sarcastic laugh. “Yes,” he said, “much too much.”

Patton remained silent, feeling his brother would speak again when he was ready. Some length of time passed while Patton listened to the cicadas and tried not to think about how much he loved Dora. He wanted to devote his full attention to Watson, but some of it always strayed back to her; she was never far gone from his mind.

When finally his brother did speak, the words were not what Patton expected. “Polly never slid,” he said simply.

“What?”

“She didn’t fall, Pat. She came at you on purpose there in the cave.”

“Why would she do that?”

Watson shook his head. “I don’t think she meant to hit you. I think it was Miss Cornett she was aiming herself at. But you got in the way.”

Patton couldn’t believe what he was hearing. Would Polly really do such a desperate thing? “What makes you think that?”

"She thought I wasn't looking, but I saw her position herself and take off flying. I saw the venom in her eyes when she did it. Only one thing could put that kind of venom there. Jealously. Plain and simple." He paused and stared into the now-dark night sky. "She never loved me."

"That's not true. She did love you."

"No. She just told me. It was always you she loved."

Patton's blood was cold. No woman could be so cruel. Heartless.

"When we got back, I told her I loved her and I'd marry her if she wanted, but I could never be a husband to her because of what had happened in the war."

Patton raised an eyebrow. Nothing had happened to Watson in the war except the illness. It certainly didn't mean he couldn't marry.

"She looked as if I'd struck her. Then I laughed at my little joke on her and told her what I'd seen. She really lost it then. Started spouting off about how she never cared a fig for me and just wanted to make you jealous. Said she wished it had been Miss Cornett that went tumbling over that rail because she was so stupid she'd never have found her way back up."

Anger threatened to explode in Patton's breast, and he thought if Polly had been there he would have stuck her—woman or not. That conniving bitch!

"Calm yourself, Pat. She's not worth the energy."

Watson seemed to be more at rest since he'd told his story. As he anger quieted somewhat, Patton felt grief for his brother. That he'd been so used and tossed aside.

Watson apparently read his mind. "Don't worry about it. I'm not." He laughed. "Remember, I'm the one who used to used to toy with them. It's a bit of turnabout, I reckon."

"She wasn't deserving of you," Patton assured him. "You'll do better."

"Maybe so. If I can outlast this illness. No matter though." Watson nudged at Patton's sore ribs. "I'll see my happiness in you and Miss Cornett. That'll do just fine."

Patton doubted it, but if it made Watson happy to

think so, he knew he would do his damnedest to be the happiest man on God's green earth. And it wouldn't be too hard, either.

The Wedding

Patton dreaded this calling on Mr. Cornett. In the past, he'd never let it bother him that Dora's father didn't care for him, but now, suddenly, it seemed imperative that the man not only give him an affirmative answer to his request, but bless their union as well. He'd tried once already to talk to Mr. Cornett, but the store had been especially busy that day and he knew it wasn't a good time to be making a request like the one he needed to make. He couldn't put it off any longer though. Though he'd thought it would kill him he'd waited patiently over the past few months for Dora to finish her schooling. They'd continued their courting, but now with her full cooperation. He'd given her the chance to see what she could have, whichever way she chose to go, but now the choices were all behind her— Patton knew they both wanted to begin the new year as man and wife.

A couple of boys were running around the yard, playing a game of war as he walked up. He wondered where in the world children got the notion that war was a game. Certainly no one returning from the battlefield would convey it as such. He thought sadly of Watson again, ill for the rest of his life because of his time served in the Philippines. It wasn't fair. And it wasn't fair that Polly Caudill had used his brother for such dire contrivings. That certainly hadn't helped Watson's outlook on the future at all. Patton prayed for him every night, that peace would come, that he would find someone worthy of him.

Of course, Polly hadn't dared to show her face on this side of the mountain since the incident at the cave. He'd written Dora a brief note saying Polly and Watson had had a falling out, and that their brief romance seemed to be ended. He knew Dora was puzzled by his refusal to say more, but he wouldn't darken her heart with the sad truth of that tale.

"Hello there, Mr. Caudill. How are you this fine day?"

At least Mary Jane Cornett always seemed glad to see him, he thought as Dora's mother waved from the porch. Even though he hadn't been able to see her cow to the market that one time she'd asked him. She wasn't one to hold a grudge.

"I'm fine, Miz Cornett. Is Mr. Cornett about?"

Mary Jane gave him a knowing smile. "That he is. Inside the store." She winked at him, a strange thing for her to do, he thought. "Tis quiet today, too. You'll have better luck."

Patton knew his reluctance must be written all over his face, because she patted his arm when he went by. "Dora's upstairs if you want to see her later," she continued, and he nodded silently as he went to wage the greatest battle he'd yet to face.

November 30, 1904

My darling one:

I have been constructing all manner of air castles for the future and in the completion—the same girl is always in the cupola. Now who do you guess this girl is?

You surely have guessed right for I certainly do love those flitting blushes that have nestled around my little time keeper so clearly, that at times it seems to be so completely hypnotized by their playfulness that it forgets there are but two living people on the face of our wonderful world.

Sorry to say I backed out square when I approached the old man this morning. Will you ever pardon me for holding you in suspense so long?

Suppose I just register Mr. Cornett a letter and ask for you? Would that suit you? You loved me before you even saw me, did you? And haven't loved me any since?

So many foolish questions.

Well, a happy goodbye.
Yours truly,
P.C.

It turned out not to be so difficult after all. As he and Dora sat on the porch swing, he marveled at how easy the task had actually been.

"You mean, he just said, 'Fine with me, boy,' and that's it? I can't believe it after all the grief he's been giving me," Dora said with amazement. "You'd have thought our marrying would be the end of the world."

"Maybe your mama talked to him?" Patton still couldn't quite believe his good fortune himself.

Dora shook her head. "Maybe. But my mama's not one to meddle."

Patton squeezed her hand. "I'm just glad he's accepted us." He brought her fingers to his mouth and kissed each one tenderly. "Soon you'll be mine."

Her eyes glowed back at him with love and some slightly out of focus something else; he wasn't quite sure but he hoped it was passion.

Patton was so happy he could burst. Barely two weeks until they wed. Dora, thank the Lord, wanted a simple wedding without a lot of fuss. He knew there'd be fuss anyway; there always was, but he was glad this was to be a quick engagement. They'd tarried too long, he thought. Time to get about their life together.

Dora was to wear Mary Jane's dress, because there wouldn't be time to make one of her own. Not that she minded; she'd always loved her mama's wedding dress. She remembered when she was a little girl, she'd spent hours just staring at the portrait of her mother and father over the fireplace. The likenesses weren't particularly good because it had been done in a hurry, but somehow, the artist had managed to capture the dress with its delicate embroidered flowers and graceful lines.

While Mary Jane tucked and pinned, Dora marveled that she and her mother had been so close to the same size at one time. Now, Mary Jane's weight had overtaken her small stature and she looked tired and worn, hardly a woman in the prime of her life. Dora shook off the fears casting about for a way back into her heart. None of that mattered now. She was going to be Patton's wife and she intended to be happy. That was that.

Her mother cleared her throat slightly and Dora looked down from the stool on which she was perched. "Yes, Mam?"

"Time I told you about your duties, child," her mother said, careful not to place too much emphasis on any of the words. Dora wanted to giggle. Did her mother really think she didn't know about all that? With seven sisters?

She held herself in check though, interested in her mother's point of view on the subject of marital relations. Somehow, she couldn't picture her mother and father ever touching in so intimate a manner. But, she supposed, most children probably felt the same way about their parents.

"He'll come to you," her mother went on, "and if you lay still and quiet, it'll soon be over. And when you're with child he'll more than likely leave you be. That's about all there is to it."

"But isn't there supposed to be some enjoyment, Ma? When Patton kisses me, I always feel there must be more to it. You mean there isn't?" Dora was disappointed. She'd hoped to find pleasure of some sort in Patton's arms. But if what her mother said was true, the whole act wasn't going to amount to much.

"Some women may find pleasure in it, daughter, but pleasure is not the point. Children are the point. That's all the good Lord wants. I suspect you'll be much happier if you don't go looking for more than that."

Mary Jane's pursed mouth was good indication that she'd said as much as she meant to on the matter. Dora, however, was not about to let the subject rest here. She couldn't believe she was about to wed and there would be no joy in the physical joining. There must be something more and she intended to find out. After all, she had 7 sisters, didn't she? Surely one of them knew better.

Dora was about to give up her quest for knowledge when her answer came from a most unexpected source. She'd discussed it with all her sisters, and they all agreed there was nothing much to enjoy—for a woman, anyway—when a man and woman joined. Dora simply could not believe that none of them had ever gotten any pleasure from the act of union. Hadn't they ever felt passion; hadn't their blood been stirred by their lover's touch? But no, they each, one by one, claimed not.

Then she was talking to her friend Stella, and Stella —shy, modest, Stella, of all people—claimed to know different. Stella, who stayed on solid ground while they'd all gone down into the pitch black cavern, proved to have a lighthearted sense of adventure after all. Who would have suspected it?

"You know Charles and I cannot marry until he gets his business more established," she told Dora. "But one night, we were having a late evening picnic by the lake, and it just happened." She squeezed Dora's arm and blushed profusely. "I can't believe I'm telling you this. I swore I'd never tell anyone."

Dora, on the other hand, could not believe her friend had been able to keep such a secret. "So, what was it like? Stella...was it horrible?"

Stella lowered her eyes shyly, then looked up at Dora from beneath thick lashes. "Hardly," she replied. "Dora, it was wonderful. It was perfect. Like something straight from a tale of romance. I can't quite explain it I'm sure...but, it's a building and building and building of such joy, that suddenly, you just feel you could explode with it—and then you do! Does that make sense?"

Dora wasn't sure it did, but that didn't matter. She'd find out for herself soon enough. And she knew

January 3, 1905

My Own Dora:

This cold snowy morning while the wind is whistling snowdrifts and icebergs through the chimney tops, it is an absolute pleasure to me to find myself scribbling a reply to your sweet missive.

I didn't back down the second time, did I dear? Your Papa's answer pleased me so well, I haven't ceased thanking him yet.

Now, if it pleases you to name the happiest day of our natural lives, I will be with you for the entertainment and not return to Sandlick until My Own can accompany me. Am I a reasonable man, Dora?

Oh! Had I only the wings of an Eagle to Dora's dainty home I would fly tonight.

Does every lady of Harlan County know that you are mine? Three good squeezes and a dozen kisses and a happy goodbye for today.

Lovingly yours,
Patton

one thing for sure: If shy demure Stella could find passion and excitement in the arms of plain boring Mr. Smusby, Dora would bet a silver dollar she could find it with Patton! Even now, the thought of it brought tingles to her insides. How could she have been so afraid? she wondered. When life was going to be such an adventure?"

The days were flying by, but for Patton, not fast enough. Every day he had to pass waiting for his bride to be his own was one day too long. He guessed he must be the luckiest man in the whole world right now. The idea that in less than one week he would bring Dora home to his parents house made his heart sing.

Patton looked around his small room, dimly lit with the golden glow of his oil lantern. Not that he didn't wish he had his own place. He'd love for them to have some privacy as they began their life together, but his little room out back would have to do for now. He had plans for their future—and those plans involved his saving money right now. Besides, Dora would be a big help to his mother with both Pa and Watson down a good bit of the time.

The thought of Watson made him frown, however. Ever since the incident with Polly, his brother had slipped into more and more of a depression. His ill health seemed as much mental as physical these days. Patton wished he could find that Polly Caudill and wring her good for nothing neck—still, what good would that do? Couldn't change what was done already, could it?

Patton went to the window and looked out into the cloudless night. He hoped it would snow on their wedding day. The last snow had melted already, and left a muddy brown world in its wake. Patton loved the snow and hoped they would have a fresh coat before the wedding. Since he wasn't about to wait to marry until the weather warmed and the sun shone full bright, he wanted as much light as possible on the day of their union. Light was how he loved seeing her best. Light was how they'd begun. The pure white snow would give him that. Dora would surely be in white as well, and he could think of no fitter thing for his virginal bride than having the day itself costumed just f

or her.

There was much William Cornett wanted to say to his daughter. As the days passed, he watched her carefully, helping her mother sew things for her hope chest, gathering the items she would soon take to her new home. He watched as she laughed and smiled little smiles to herself as if she had some sweet secret.

Little did she know most of the rest of the world had known this secret as well—and had come to discover, after time, it wasn't so sweet.

He sighed. He had tried so hard to protect his daughters. To give them more. A chance for a different sort of life than the one their mother had known. One by one, he'd watched them all go to their marriages, just as Mary Jane herself had done. William swore if he'd known the toll life was to take on his wife, he'd never have married her to begin with. He'd have left her there with her father, alone but perhaps happier. Better alone than wasted, he thought now.

What could he say to Dora? He'd done his talking before. He'd made his pleas; he'd given her the chances. Now she was to go to her future without him at her side. She would go into another man's keeping. But Dora didn't know this. She saw herself going into freedom, where man and wife would be equal in love. Humpf, he thought, there was no equality in love or life. Not for women.

Dora came out onto the porch, bundled up, and sat down beside him on the swing. It was too cold to be out, and she must be wondering what bid him to come and sit in the chilly weather like this?

"Papa? Aren't you freezing?"

She was still such a girl, he thought as he looked at her. Still only a child. Probably, her mother had told her nothing about the ways of men and women. Would Patton be gentle? Shh...it was not for him to be wondering such things, was it?

William patted his daughter's arm, reassuring her. "How are things, daughter? Is your trousseau ready for tomorrow?"

She nodded, and he couldn't ignore the light in her eyes. She was certainly happy, he'd grant that. And he was partly to thank for this happiness.

"Papa, you aren't upset are you? About my decision?" A small anxious look came over her face. She loved him; he was certain of that. And God, how he did love her! His beautiful young daughter.

"No, no, Doe. I am not upset with you." He put his arms around her and held her quite close to his heart for a long time, gathering in her warmth and pouring his love back to her.

Finally, he set her back and met her sweet eyes. "Be happy, my dear," he told her softly. "Be happy, and try never to be disappointed. Life often holds disappointments we don't expect. You'll promise me this?"

She squeezed his hand. "I promise, Papa. I will be happy. I will."

He returned her smile, knowing such a promise was pointless indeed. But all the same, wishing her well.

She woke that morning with a heart filled near to bursting with joy. She had never known she could feel such joy. This was the day she'd been waiting for. This was her wedding day.

Dora jumped out of bed and ran to the window. It was snowing. Light delicate flakes made lacy trails across the window pane. Patton had wanted snow, she knew. He would be happy. Somehow, it made her even happier to think of Patton there at home, his heart singing because of the snow. And her.

She looked around the room. This was the last morning she would ever wake up in this room as a girl. Her favorite things were already gone—the wedding ring quilt, the white porcelain pitcher and vase, her books, her pictures—all packed away to go to the home of her husband. If she ever slept in her father's house again, it would not be as his innocent daughter, but as the wife of another man. As a true woman.

Tonight, all mysteries would be known, and tomorrow... tomorrow would be the first day of her new life. Dora couldn't wait.

Mary Jane Wynn watched it all with a mother's eyes. Those eyes saw both the beauty and the sadness. They knew that this was the last day of her daughter's youth —from henceforth everything would be viewed with knowledge; innocence was no more.

The scene had the look of a painting, she thought, with all its stark and icy majesty. She remembered the church in Springtime, and felt melancholy that her daughter couldn't have been married when everything was fresh and in bloom. Marrying in the dead of winter seemed odd to her. Still, there was a purity to the snowy white mountains that was perhaps appropriate for a virgin bride.

Sitting now, waiting for her daughter to come down the aisle of the little church with her father, Mary Jane remembered how happy Dora had looked this morning, with her faded silk and winter flowers in her hair. The sisters had all been there to help, for marriages were a time of family communion—they too had had that blessing at their unions. They'd fussed and fretted and made Dora beautiful, more beautiful than she'd ever been or perhaps ever would be again. On this day Dora Cornett was truly queen of the world...

Mary Jane sighed. Unfortunately, tomorrow would come all too soon.

The door opened, and the little church was flooded with light. Light from the sun; light reflected off the snow; light from the pure beauty of her. The light caught the silk of her dress, and he remembered the first time he'd seen her.

Patton had often wondered if this day would ever come, and now that it was here, he wanted it to last forever. He watched as she moved in slow motion toward him. Everything else was a blur. Nothing here — no one—except her.

It seemed an eternity before she reached the place where he stood, right next to God, waiting patiently for his own slice of heaven. When she was almost there, he found her eyes, glowing with joy, glowing with love.

Patton held out his hand. She reached out and took it, and he melted inside as he sensed the velvety softness of her skin through her white cotton glove. She took his hand, and the magic became real.

Biographical Note

Dora Cornett married Samuel Patton Caudill on January 14, 1905. They had 8 children, born within a span of 11 years. In 1908 Patton took his family to New Mexico territory to farm, only to discover he had purchased a piece of desert wasteland. Rather than return to a depressed Kentucky however, he settled them in Ardmore, Oklahoma, where Patton provided as best he could. Samuel Patton Caudill died of a heart attack in his late forties.

Dora Cornett Caudill never remarried. She lived to the age of 83, and was well-loved and much-respected by her descendants.

www.ingramcontent.com/pod-product-compliance
Ingram Content Group UK Ltd.
Pitfield, Milton Keynes, MK11 3LW, UK
UKHW041846190726
13854UKWH00002B/740